Balance of Power

☩

Balance of Power

a cautionary tale.

by

Dr JL Iddon

First Published in 2019 by Dr JL Iddon

ISBN: 9781092678063

Disclaimer:
This is entirely a work of fiction. Any apparent similarity with any person in real life is entirely coincidental.

This book is dedicated to my boys Milo, Luke & Ned and to the generations they represent.

May they all choose to live by this motto:

CARE, BE FAIR, AND SHARE

About the style of writing in this book

To write a book, you have to have enough continuous time in your life, so as not to break the 'flow'. The theme of Virginia Woolf's "A Room of One's Own" (1929) specifically refers to the household chores that constrain women writers. It should of course be very different now, with women being educated 'as equals' alongside men. But infact, be enlarge, the lions share of organisation around family and household is still done by women, often alongside a busy job. So the prospect of ever being able to finish a full length book, whether as a writer or indeed a reader, are slim.

And so his book is written instead more in the style of a darkly humorous story, along the lines of Hans Christian Anderson & Hilaire Belloc, but with a touch of Pam Ayres. It is intended to have flow and fast tempo but to be short and sweet. Above all else it is natural and straightforward, intended to get a clear message across in an easy read thought provoking format to the reader.

Modern writing for busy times.

CONTENTS

PROLOGUE

This is a philosophical tale about a family's life. All starts out fine when it's just husband and wife. But over time as the family starts to grow, traditional maleness starts to show.

Be warned the tone is quite intense, and it's not a light-hearted story in any sense. But what it does is give stark insight, into modern issues that need to be put right.

PART 1

This is a warning story to you all. A husband from his pedestal did fall. Because of him his life derailed, and his happy family all but failed. It started well, but when the babes were born, she adapted, but he just would not transform.

Years went by but nothing changed, their relationship became increasingly strained. She had more and more and more to do, yet she was working full time too. She simply couldn't understand his rigid stance,

"You nag" he'd say. "Help you? Not a chance!"

She valiantly struggled on and on, growing more fatigued each day. Juggling work, the house & children all alone led to burnout and dismay. At first she'd been like 'supermum', but over time that changed. She was holding on by her fingernails, and they were becoming increasingly estranged.

Doing just too much for far too long, and him not helping one bit, was clearly wrong, yet on top of that, he became an increasingly grumpy shit!

It was relentless stress and pressure, alongside working in her busy professional role. Doing everything for everyone else, insidiously took it's toll.

And whilst he climbed the ladder, she gave up more and more to cope. Her energy sapped, no time for herself, she tried hard not to mope. She thought he just didn't understand, that it was hard coping as a one-girl band.

"I have to go to work," he'd say, not seeming to clock that she was increasingly feeling blue. He simply failed to even acknowledge, that she was working too!

But she thought at least he had one saving grace, that together forever life they would face. And so she stalwartly kept her faith in him, believing that despite his failings, he was there for her within.

And so she simply soldiered on, and on, and on, and on, and on and on.

11

PART 2

Until one day she came across a text message - one that caused her very serious dismay. It turned out that he was more than just an unhelpful chap.....he had been having an affair on top of that........having fun and making hay.

Finding this out was an utter seismic shock. Gone......just like that was her apparent rock. Looking back it was rather sadly clear, he hadn't held them quite so dear. In fact not only had he failed to help her out at all, he had actually engineered her fall. Yet she had never even doubted him, he hadn't seemed the type to sin.

Whilst he'd been rubbish at being a modern man, she had resolutely remained his faithful fan. But that all changed the day she found, that he had also been sleeping around.

But back to the moment she saw his phone, in shock at that message with the clearly sexual overtone. She remained calm and simply put his keys away, for she new their relationship was over that day.

He didn't know what she had seen, what he had done, where he had been, and when he went out to collect his shirts, she hid how much she had been hurt.

He couldn't work out where his keys had gone, but she smiled sweetly, sad at her necessary con.

"I will let you in when you get back," she said. But inside she was devastated and seeing red.

On his return he rang the bell, but through the door a message fell. It was simply a piece of paper plain and written on it was his lovers name…..

All went quiet…..she heard him walk away, there was really nothing he could say. The children cried but she said of him,

"Daddy's been naughty, we will not let him in."

That was the day that marked the end of this couples love, an instant guillotine, caused by the above. It was the final straw, that was it. Having an affair on top of not helping one bit. It was really unforgivable what he had done, but now the dark set in, gone was the sun.

PART 3

The moral of this tale, I'm sure is clear - it was
he alone that tore apart their family dear. By
refusing to help, indulging in his needless lust,
all that had once been, was turned to dust. But
much worse than that he'd watched her fail,
remaining a resolutely traditional male. Whilst
equal once, he just refused to adapt, made her
feel sad, lonely and trapped.

So the basic message to any similar-minded
guy…. your girl will be happier the more you
try. It is simply about the effort that you make,
care be fair and share…. before it's too late.

Offer your help, or just muck in, share the
cooking, empty the bin. Use your brain to
make weekends fun, think about the children,
and love their mum. Help her think and help
her do, frankly….really….why wouldn't you?

But it isn't just the guys you know, the girls are
inadvertently causing this too. By doing too
much, giving up work, you are fuelling the
traditional view.

Girl's easily succumb to the roles they have learnt, and that is partly why so many are getting burnt. But it's important that you too make a stand, start to insist your man gives you more of a hand. Because if only a few females ask of this, they are branded feminists and are easy to diss.

But thats just bullshit - a convenient line, to get out of sharing most of the time. It's not about women taking control, its simply about having a dual role. It's about catching up with the times we are in. It's about every one of us in a balanced win - win.

Each and every girl and boy needs to see, how important it is both she and he, pull their weight in equal measure, it's only then life can become more of a pleasure.

It's not about one and not the other - it's about every girl and boy, sister and brother, caring enough and choosing to share. The bottom line is it's about being fair…..

Lets work towards creating a world

where everybody thrives.

Bring a balance of power

to all of our lives.

EPILOGUE

Times have changed, but the problem for you, is that what you say is not what you do. And that's an important message for all to clock, because to close that gap you must remove that block. Stop repeating the same patterns over and over again. Choose to adapt and evolve - both women and men.

Choose to change, choose to share, respect each other, just be fair. Because now 50% of marriages end in strife and that really truly will devastate your life. Wouldn't it be better to work as a team? Not become estranged and start to be mean. There is so much bitter anger out there - but for your children's sake - choose to be fair.

There's a clear reason, surely it's easy to see, and each person individually holds the key. The one that opens the new world door.....so lets choose to evolve and end the underlying gender war.

POSTSCRIPT

But there is just one more thing I have to say, it's really about the next generation of kids at the end of the day. Parents - you are their role models, but frankly your not doing great. They will learn from you and in due course, will experience the exact same fate.

Unless adults choose to change their ways, one day those kids will enter the same difficult gender imbalance maze. But wouldn't it really be rather nice, if way more adults passed down updated advice?

Because then the younger generations would have a chance to really change, and that's when the world will move on from being stuck in this twilight phase.

So when the kids come home from school each day, instead of following the traditional rules, they could instead help their parents, start to develop useful real world practical tools.

Homework could be learning to cook, and doing even just one household chore. Maybe emptying the dishwasher, or hoovering the kitchen floor. Rather than switching on the telly, or going straight onto their Ipads, how about preparing all your kids to become fairer mums and dads?

We live within a system, where what we choose to think and do, influences the children, who in the future will behave exactly like that too.

So please just take a moment to reflect upon your daily life, and let me ask the question, are you a happy man and wife? Do you both work and share the childcare? Do you live fair and balanced lives? Or are you more reminiscent of the couple here - i.e. wife struggles while husband thrives?

It's time to ask those questions, get really honest with yourselves. Because unlike the tale of the shoemaker, there really are no elves. Your children are at your mercy - and it's time for you to face, that it's collectively you parents who will determine, the future of the human race.....

THE END

About the Author

Dr Joanna Lucy Iddon is a British cognitive behavioural neuropsychologist. She is a published academic papers & chapters, and has written several books on memory.   She is regularly interviewed as an expert on radio, television and for newspaper and magazine articles. Dr Iddon lives in london with her three children.   This is her first cautionary tale....

Printed in Great Britain
by Amazon